Lucky Star that shines so bright,
Who will need your help tonight?
Light up the sky, it's thanks to you
Wishes really do come true . . .

Lucky Stars

Explore the sparkling world of the stars at
www.luckystarsbooks.co.uk

Wishes really do come true

Lucky Stars

The Birthday Wish

Phoebe Bright

Illustrated by Karen Donnelly

MACMILLAN CHILDREN'S BOOKS

A Working Partners book

With special thanks to Maria Faulkner

First published 2012 by Macmillan Children's Books

This edition published 2013 by Macmillan Children's Books
a division of Macmillan Publishers Limited
20 New Wharf Road, London N1 9RR
Basingstoke and Oxford
Associated companies throughout the world
www.panmacmillan.com

ISBN 978-1-4472-0249-3

Printed and bound by CPI Group (UK) Ltd, Croydon CR0 4YY

With thanks to all the magical people
in my life for their belief in me

Contents

Hello, friend!

I'm Stella Starkeeper and I want to tell you a secret. Have you ever gazed up at the stars and thought how magical they looked? Well, you're right. Stars really do have magic!

Their precious glittering light allows me to fly down from the sky, all the way to Earth. You see, I'm always on the lookout for boys and girls who are especially kind and helpful. I train them to become Lucky Stars - people who can make wishes come true!

So the next time you're under the twinkling night sky, look out for me. I'll be floating among the stars somewhere. Do give me a wave!

Love from
Stella x

1
The Great Fandango

'Snap!' said Cassie, putting a matching card on the pile. 'I'm going to win this time.'

'We'll see about that,' said Alex. He grinned and put down another card.

It was a rainy day in Astral-on-Sea. Cassie and Alex were playing a game of Snap in her bedroom at Starwatcher Towers. Cassie's parents owned the Starwatcher Towers Bed and Breakfast, and Alex was there on holiday with his family, including his little white puppy, Comet. Alex and Cassie had become firm friends.

'SNAP!' Alex shouted. 'That's two games to me and one to you. You see, it's all about probability.'

'Probability?' Cassie repeated.

'It's a theory scientists use to work out how often something might happen,' Alex replied. 'I'm working out how often the cards come up in pairs by counting the cards in between.'

Cassie smiled. Only Alex would know a scientific way to play Snap.

'I think you're just lucky!' she said.

She looked up at the glass roof of her bedroom and sighed. It curved round into a dome shape just like the roof of her dad's observatory. At night, Cassie liked watching the stars through the glass roof, but now all she could see were raindrops falling with a steady pitter-pat.

'It's raining too hard to go out,' she said,

stroking Twinkle, her old black cat. He purred happily. 'What if someone's making a wish? How will I know if I'm stuck indoors?' she wondered aloud.

'You've already helped make three people's wishes come true,' Alex pointed out. 'So the probability is that you'll somehow manage to help a fourth person.'

Twinkle nuzzled Cassie's arm and the charms on her bracelet tinkled together. Stella Starkeeper, Cassie's magical friend, had given her the silver bracelet for her seventh birthday a few days before. Every time Cassie helped to make someone's wish come true, she received another charm with a new magical power. So far, she had four charms – with the bird charm she could fly, with the crescent moon she could speak to animals, and with the butterfly she could freeze time. Her newest charm was a flower, but she didn't know yet what its magic power was. When she earned seven charms she would become a real Lucky Star, like Stella. Then she would be able to grant any wish she liked! But Cassie knew she had a lot to do before that magical day.

Cassie looked at the grey sky. There
was no sign of Stella Starkeeper among the
clouds.

She heard Alex's tummy growl noisily.

'I'm hungry,' he said.

'I'm hungry too,' Cassie agreed. 'Let's go
and get some breakfast.'

Cassie carried Twinkle downstairs to the
dining room where she and Alex tucked
into boiled eggs and toast.

'I wonder if it will ever stop raining
today,' Cassie said with a sigh.

'Ahem,' a new voice chipped in. 'May I
join you? I think I could make your grey
day disappear!'

Cassie turned round in surprise to see
who had spoken. There stood a boy, a little

taller than Alex, wearing a top hat and a black cape. He gave them a cheeky grin. Cassie recognized him as one of the new bed-and-breakfast guests.

'Yes, of course you can join us,' Cassie said. 'I'm Cassie and this is Alex.'

The new boy bowed and his shiny black cape swung around his shoulders, revealing a bright red lining.

'I am the Great Fandango,' he announced.

'That's a very unusual name,' Alex said.

'My real name's Marcus Chen,' Marcus told them. 'The Great Fandango is my stage name. I chose "Fandango" because it sounds magical, and "Great" because that's what I want my tricks to be.'

'You're a magician!' Cassie said excitedly.

'Yes,' said Marcus.

'I'm going to be a scientist,' said Alex.

'Wow,' Marcus said, 'that's *great* too.'

Cassie and Alex laughed.

'Why have you got your magician's outfit on?' Alex asked.

'I'm doing a magic show at my cousin Lia's birthday party,' Marcus explained. 'She's five today. I don't see her very often because we live far away. The magic show is my birthday present to her.'

'What a brilliant idea,' Alex said.

'Do you like magic?' asked Marcus.

Cassie and Alex grinned at one another.
They certainly liked the magical adventures
they had using the charms on Cassie's
bracelet.

'We love magic,' Cassie said.

With a flourish, Marcus pulled out a

black wand with a white tip. 'Then I shall show you my magic tricks,' he said.

He turned the bottom of Alex's empty eggshell upside down on the plate. Then he shook out a clean napkin and carefully covered the empty shell.

As she watched Marcus prepare his trick, Cassie noticed a glimmer of sunshine through the dining-room window. It made the streaks of rainwater on the windows gleam like diamonds.

This could turn out to be quite a magical day after all, she thought with a smile.

2
Magic Tricks

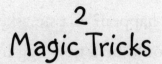

Marcus slowly waved his wand over the
napkin that covered the eggshell then
tapped it three times. Whoosh! He whipped
the napkin away. All three children peered at
the shell.

Apart from a bit of a crack, it looked
exactly the same.

'Oops,' Marcus
said.

'Was something

supposed to happen?' Cassie asked.

'There should be a new egg in its place,' Marcus explained.

He tapped the eggshell again. Nothing happened.

'I suppose the yolk's on me,' he said.

Cassie and Alex giggled.

'Try another trick,' said Cassie. 'You just need to keep practising.'

Marcus nodded in agreement. 'The Great Fandango never gives up!' he said.

He pointed his wand at the scarf that Cassie was wearing.

'Would you mind if I borrowed your scarf?' he asked.

'Not at all,' Cassie replied. As she untied the scarf and gave it to Marcus, the silver moons and stars on it sparkled.

'It looks magical!' he said.

'Thank you,' Cassie replied.

'I'll place the scarf up my sleeve. And when I wave my wand I'll produce one hundred scarves!' Marcus explained.

He waved his wand in the air then reached inside his sleeve. He frowned slightly.

Oh dear, Cassie thought. *The trick's gone wrong again. Poor Marcus.*

Marcus looked up his sleeve and slowly pulled out – Cassie's scarf!

'That's odd,' he said. 'There's supposed to be a string of scarves all knotted together.'

He lowered his arm and a plastic egg dropped out of the sleeve!

Marcus opened his eyes and mouth wide, pulling the funniest of surprised faces and Cassie and Alex burst out laughing.

'Well,' he said, 'at least I found the egg!'

'Oh, Marcus,' Cassie giggled. 'You're so funny!'

'But not a very good magician,' he said sadly. 'I've got *lots* of practising to do this morning if I'm going to make Lia's birthday party special.'

He gave a bow, swirled his cape and

walked out of the dining room.

'I'd better get going too,' Alex said. 'It's stopped raining and I promised to take Comet for a walk. Do you want to come?'

'I'll just help Dad clear the guests' breakfast dishes,' Cassie replied. 'I'll see you later.'

'OK,' Alex said, and dashed off to find his puppy's lead.

Twinkle meowed loudly at Cassie as if he was trying to tell her something.

'One moment, Twinkle.' Cassie concentrated hard on the crescent moon charm until silver sparkles swirled around it and her furry cat.

'Now I can understand you,' said Cassie. 'What were you saying, Twinkle?'

21

'That boy is funnier than a dog chasing its tail!' Twinkle meowed.

'Marcus is funny,' Cassie agreed. 'He really wants to be a magician and do magic tricks, but he keeps getting them wrong.' She looked at her pretty flower charm. 'I wonder if my new charm has the power to help him?'

The Birthday Wish

'I think he'll need a lot of help,' Twinkle
said, batting the plastic egg under the table.
'But I like him even if his tricks don't
work.'

'Me too.' Cassie laughed as she began
piling the breakfast plates on to a tray. She
had just picked up the last plate when she
spotted a dazzling
orb of light
shooting across
the sky.

Twinkle spotted
it too and bolted
under one of the
dining chairs.

'Dad,' Cassie
called into the

kitchen, 'can I go out and play now?'

'Of course,' her dad replied. 'Thanks for your help.'

Cassie ran outside, following the spinning star. It flew down the sloping hill towards the apple orchard.

With a *whizz* and a *fizz* and a *zip-zip-zip*, the star zoomed over the orchard. It slowed and hovered by one particular tree. Cassie watched as it grew into a column of dazzling light, which slowly changed into Stella Starkeeper!

Wearing her glittering dress, neat little jacket and shiny leggings, Stella sat on a branch swinging her silvery boots back and forth.

'It's lovely to see you,' Cassie said,

scrambling up the tree and giving Stella a
big hug.

'You've been very busy,' Stella said,
touching the new flower charm on Cassie's
bracelet. 'You've got your fourth charm,
Cassie. Well done!'

Cassie felt very proud.

'Only three more charms to earn, Cassie,
and then you'll be a Lucky Star – just like
me,' said Stella.

She tapped the little flower charm. Cassie
gasped as the
charm burst into
a bunch of flowers
before becoming
a single flower
again.

The Birthday Wish

'How did you do that?' Cassie asked.

'I'll give you a clue,' Stella said with a smile. 'Sometimes things appear out of thin air.'

Then, in a cascade of glittering sparkles, she disappeared.

Sometimes things appear out of thin air, Cassie thought. *Hmm, what does that mean?*

3
Disappearing Magician

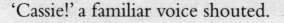

'Cassie!' a familiar voice shouted.

Through the trees, Cassie saw Alex. Comet was scampering on the end of his lead.

'Hi,' Alex said, running over. 'Your mum asked if we would collect the cupcakes she ordered from the Fairy-cake Bakery.'

'Oh, lovely,' Cassie said, scrambling down from the branch. 'We might see Kate there.'

Kate was Cassie's friend and her mum

owned the bakery. Kate often helped make
the cakes and biscuits.

Cassie, Alex and Comet walked down the
hill and along the sea front. Cassie looked
around, trying to spot someone who might
need her help. There were lots of people
walking along the promenade, and on the
beach children were building sandcastles
and splashing in the waves. Everyone looked
perfectly happy, enjoying
the sunshine after the
morning's rain.

I can't see anyone
who needs to
make a wish,
thought
Cassie.

The Birthday Wish

When they reached the bakery, Cassie drew a deep breath as the wonderful smell of cakes and biscuits filled the air.

'Comet, I think we'd better wait outside,' said Alex.

Cassie laughed at the little puppy, who was gazing longingly through the bakery window. Inside, the shop bustled with people buying the gorgeous pastries, buns and cakes that lined the shelves. Cassie could see Kate and her mum busily serving the customers.

Cassie joined the queue behind a cheerful-looking lady carrying lots of bags and boxes.

'I've come to collect a birthday cake,' the lady said when it was her turn. 'It's for my

daughter,
Lia. She's
turning five
today.'
Cassie
realized the lady was Marcus's auntie. *The
cake must be for his cousin's party*, she thought,
where Marcus is going to do his magic show.

'Hello, Mrs Chen,' Kate's mum said.

'You're a bit early and I'm afraid it isn't quite ready yet.'

She pointed to a beautiful pink-and-white cake, covered in delicate flowers and five silver star-shaped candles. A marzipan fairy castle lay next to the cake, along with some sparkly fairies made from sugar.

'The icing has to set completely before the fairy decorations can go on,' she explained.

'I do understand,' Mrs Chen said, looking flustered. 'But I have so many things to do for Lia's birthday party that I don't know when I can come back.'

'Excuse me,' Cassie said. 'My name's
Cassie. Marcus is staying with us at
Starwatcher Towers and he told us about
Lia's party. Perhaps my friend Alex and I
could collect the cake for you. I could ask
my mum to come in the car.'

The Birthday Wish

'That's very kind of you, Cassie,' Mrs Chen said. 'Are you sure your mum won't mind?'

'I'm sure,' said Cassie. Her parents were always offering to help the guests at the B & B.

'Thank you,' said Mrs Chen. 'Would you and Alex like to come to the party? It's in the garden of Flashley Manor Hotel.'

'We'd love to – thank you!' Cassie replied. But inside her heart sank. *I hope Donna Fox doesn't try to ruin Lia's party*, she thought. Donna's parents owned Flashley Manor and Donna always liked to get her own way.

Kate had finished serving the other customers, and now ran over to Cassie with a box of cupcakes.

'They're beautiful!' said Cassie.

The cupcakes were decorated with swirls of yellow, orange and green icing and topped with shiny cherries.

'Mum's put in some extra cakes for you and Alex,' said Kate as she closed the pretty box.

'Thank you!' Cassie called to Kate's mum. She gave Cassie a smile. Waving goodbye to Kate, Cassie ran outside and joined Alex and Comet.

'We've got to come back and collect Lia's birthday cake later,' she said. 'And look – Kate's mum gave us some extra cupcakes.' She showed Alex the cakes.

'Yum!' he said. 'They look delicious.'

Comet yipped excitedly.

'He thinks so too,' laughed Alex.

'Let's take them home and share the cakes with Marcus,' Cassie said.

'Great idea,' Alex agreed. 'And we can find out if his magic tricks are getting better.'

Cassie held on tightly to the cupcake box as she and Alex ran back up the hill to Starwatcher Towers, Comet yipping all the way. They took the extra cakes to share

with Marcus and left the rest on the kitchen
table.

But where *was* Marcus? They searched all
over Starwatcher Towers. He wasn't in his
guest bedroom or in the sitting room, or
the dining room or the kitchen. They even
checked Cassie's dad's observatory and her

own bedroom at the top of the house. But there was no sign of Marcus anywhere.

'It's as if he's magically disappeared!' Cassie said.

4
Out of Thin Air!

Puzzled, Cassie and Alex sat on the doorstep
of Starwatcher Towers, wondering where
to look next. Twinkle was dozing in the
flowerbed, enjoying the sunshine. Comet
licked the old cat's ear and Twinkle opened
one sleepy eye.

'Twinkle likes to watch the guests coming
and going,' Cassie said. 'Maybe he knows
where Marcus went.'

She concentrated on her crescent moon

charm. Silver sparkles swirled around her
bracelet and around Twinkle too.

'Twinkle, have you seen Marcus?' asked
Cassie.

'I think he went to the orchard,' Twinkle
replied. 'He almost tripped over me because

of all the boxes he was carrying. I had to move off the doorstep.'

'Thanks, Twinkle,' Cassie said, giving the cat a tickle under the chin.

Leaving Comet in the garden to play with Twinkle, they ran to the orchard, searching for Marcus.

'It'll be easier to spot him if we fly,' Cassie said.

She took Alex's hand and thought about the bird charm on her bracelet. Silver sparkles danced around them and their feet lifted off the ground. *Whoosh!* Together, they flew over the trees.

Suddenly, they heard a dramatic voice below them. 'Abracadabra!'

'I think we've found him,' Cassie chuckled.

Looking down, she spotted Marcus standing on a stage made of the wooden crates that her parents used to collect juicy apples. Another box made a table. Behind Marcus, an old sheet hung between two trees to create a backdrop. Poking out from under the sheet was a colourful bag full of magic props.

'I don't think we should disturb him,' Cassie said. 'It looks like he's trying a very difficult trick.'

Cassie concentrated on her bird charm and the silver sparkles swirled around them as they dropped gently from the sky to land behind a tree.

As they watched, Marcus picked up a rather squidgy apple from the

ground and held it in the air.

'Ladies and gentlemen,' Marcus said, pretending he had an audience. 'For my next trick, I will turn this apple into an orange!'

With a flourish, he tapped a shiny black box three times and threw the apple into the air.

'Abracadabra!'

Cassie held her breath. Would the trick work?

Splat! The rotten apple came down on Marcus's head. Though he did look funny covered in squelchy apple,

The Birthday Wish

Cassie held back her laughter.

'Oh no,' Alex whispered. 'It's gone wrong again.'

Cassie knew she had to do something. She ran out from behind the tree, Alex following her.

'What a brilliant stage, Marcus!' Cassie said.

'It looks great,' Alex added.

'If only my magic act was great too,' said Marcus. The side of the box dropped open and an orange rolled out. 'That was supposed to happen earlier,' he said with a groan. 'I can't get any of my tricks right.'

Cassie knelt to pick up the orange. 'Don't give up,' she said. 'Remember, you're the Great Fandango.'

But Marcus sighed.
'Lia's going to be so
disappointed,'
he said.
'I wish I
could make her
birthday party special.'
Cassie and Alex
shared a secret smile.
Marcus had made
a wish, and it was
up to Cassie to

make sure it came true. On her wrist, the
little flower charm twinkled in the sunlight.

I need to find out what power it gives me,
she thought. *Then I can help!* Aloud, she
told Marcus, 'You will make Lia's birthday

special. You just need some practice.'

'Really?' Marcus asked.

Cassie nodded. She looked at Alex, who seemed to be frowning in concentration. 'And we'll help you, won't we?' she said.

'Of course,' Alex replied. Suddenly, he snapped his fingers. 'In fact, I've got an idea for a new trick! All we need are three cups big enough to hide a cupcake!'

Alex held a cupcake out to Marcus.

'But I haven't got any cups,' Marcus said.

Both boys looked

glumly at the props bag.

'I'll go and find some in the B & B,'
Cassie offered. 'Be right back.'

At Starwatcher Towers, Cassie
searched the kitchen cupboards. On
one of the shelves she spotted two large
mugs.

These would be perfect, she thought. *But I
need three of them! If only an extra mug would
appear.*

Without thinking, she gazed at the flower
charm on her bracelet. The flower glittered
and then burst into a bunch of flowers!
Silver sparkles swirled around the bracelet
and over the kitchen counter. *Poof!* With a
little burst of stars, a third mug appeared –
out of thin air!

The Birthday Wish

'Wow,'
Cassie said,
remembering
what Stella
Starkeeper
had said. 'So
that's what my
flower charm can do –
it makes things appear. That's the perfect
kind of magic to help a magician!'

5
Where's the Cupcake?

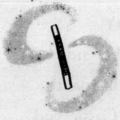

Cassie ran back to the orchard. She could hear Alex talking to Marcus.

'That sounds very scientific,' Cassie said, laying out the mugs next to the cupcake. They were just big enough to hide the cakes.

'I'm explaining the theory of probability to Marcus,' Alex said.

'Isn't that the theory you used to win Snap?' asked Cassie.

'That's right,' said
Alex.

Marcus scratched
his head. 'I don't
understand it,' he said.

'I think you'll have to
show us, Alex,' Cassie said.

'OK,' said Alex. 'I can
show you with
the cupcake
trick.'

Alex hid the
cupcake under
one of the mugs,
turned the other two
over, then moved them in figures of eight.

'Now, which mug do you think the

cupcake is under?' asked Alex.

'The one on the right,' Cassie answered.

'No, the left!' Marcus cried.

Alex lifted the two mugs but the cupcake wasn't under either of them.

'Look!' he said, lifting the middle mug to reveal the cupcake.

Cassie and Marcus clapped.

'Most people will *probably* guess the left or the right,' Alex told Marcus. 'So you must make sure the cupcake always ends up in the middle.'

'Very clever,' said Cassie.

Alex showed Marcus how to do the trick. 'Now you try,' he said.

While Marcus moved the mugs round and round, Cassie pulled Alex behind the sheet curtain.

'I've found out what my flower charm can do,' she whispered. 'Watch this.'

Cassie concentrated on her flower charm. It burst into a bunch of flowers, and sparkles swirled around her bracelet and her hand. *Poof!* A shiny green apple appeared.

'That's fantastic!' said Alex.

'Perhaps I have to make something appear out of thin air to help Marcus,' Cassie said.

'Maybe,' said Alex. 'But what?'

Just then, Marcus called, 'I think I've got it!'

Cassie and Alex ran to watch.

Marcus moved the mugs so fast that they
had no idea where the cupcake was.

'It's under the mug on the left,' Cassie
shouted.

'No, it's on the right,' Alex said.

'I'm afraid you're both wrong,' Marcus said.

With a flourish, he lifted the middle mug. But the cupcake wasn't there.

'Oops,' he said.

'Try again,' said Cassie.

Marcus tried several times but he couldn't get it right.

'Hmmm,' he said, disappointed. Then he brightened. 'Oh well, when I *do* find the cupcake, I know a trick that will make it disappear completely.'

Once more, Marcus moved the mugs round and round, but again he lost track of the cupcake. When he finally found it, he plucked the cherry off the top, and ate the rest!

'See,' he said. 'It's disappeared!'

Cassie and Alex fell about laughing. Marcus grinned and stuck the cherry on the end of his nose, making them laugh even more.

'Marcus, your tricks might go wrong, but you really know how to make people laugh,' Cassie said. 'And that's a special kind of magic.'

'But I've promised Lia that she'll get to see some proper magic tricks,' Marcus said gloomily.

'Don't give up,' Cassie said. 'Lia will love

your show. You're a magician *and* a comic, all in one!'

'Besides,' Alex piped up, 'I've found a way for you to remember where the cupcake is.' He showed them a tiny chip on one of the mug handles. 'If you always place the cupcake under the chipped mug, you'll know exactly where to find it.'

Marcus tried the trick again with another cupcake under the chipped mug. It worked! Quickly, they packed up the stage and the props, and ran back to Starwatcher Towers.

'Well, I'm as ready as I'll ever be. There's no more time to practise,' Marcus said with a sigh. 'It's almost time for Lia's party. I just hope I can remember my tricks with everyone watching.'

The Birthday Wish

Whatever happens, Cassie thought, *I have to make Marcus's wish come true and help Lia to have the best party ever!*

Cassie's mum came downstairs and took the car keys from her handbag. 'Your mum and dad are already at the party, helping to set everything up,' she explained to Marcus. 'I told them I'd drop you off.'

Lucky Stars

Cassie, Alex and Marcus piled into the car with Cassie's mum. On his lap, Marcus held his bag of props – including a cupcake.

Their first stop was the Fairy-cake Bakery to collect Lia's birthday cake.

'It's beautiful!' Cassie told Kate's mum when she saw the pink-and-white cake, now with the fairy castle and sparkly fairies on top.

'Lia's going to love it!' said Marcus.

Cassie helped her mum placed the large cake box in the boot of the car for the drive to Flashley Manor Hotel. Cassie hoped it wouldn't jiggle about too much. She wanted it to be in perfect condition for Lia.

Cassie's mum dropped them off at Flashley Manor hotel. Carefully, Cassie and

The Birthday Wish

Marcus carried the cake up the sweeping steps to the large front door, with Alex behind them, ready to catch the cake in case it fell.

The door flew open and a girl wearing a sparkly leotard and leggings glared at them.

Cassie's heart skipped a beat. It was Donna Fox.

6

A Magic Show

'Who invited *you*?' asked Donna.

'Mrs Chen. We've brought Lia's birthday cake,' Cassie said, holding the cake box out in front of her.

Cassie took a step back as Donna's blue eyes narrowed. 'And what are *they* doing here?' Donna asked, pointing to Alex and Marcus.

'Helping,' Alex mumbled.

'Marcus is Lia's cousin,' Cassie added.

'Otherwise known as the Great Fandango. He's going to do a magic show at Lia's party.'

'The Great Fandango, eh? We'll see if you're so great,' Donna snapped. 'Just remember, this is the *great* Flashley Manor

Hotel and it belongs to my parents.' With a flick of her ponytail she marched ahead of them. 'The party's through there,' she said, pointing at a white-and-gold door.

'Thank you,' Cassie said politely, but Donna had already walked away.

Cassie, Marcus and Alex walked down the thickly carpeted hallway, still carrying the birthday cake. It led to a grand room with velvet-covered furniture. Twinkling chandeliers hung from the high ceiling.

'Donna's sent us the wrong way,' Cassie said with a sigh.

At last, they found a huge conservatory with shiny glass doors that led out to the garden. Cassie's heart lifted when she saw a sparkly banner strung across the trees.

Lots of girls and boys were playing on the lawn and there were brightly coloured balloons everywhere. Marcus smiled at his mum and dad, who were talking to some of the other parents.

Cassie and Marcus placed the cake on a trestle table beside a platform that had a red curtain across it.

'Look, Marcus,' Alex said. 'This must be the stage for your magic show.'

Marcus's mouth gaped open. 'What a lot

of people,' he said. 'What if I get my tricks wrong in front of everyone?'

Just then, Mrs Chen came hurrying over. 'Hello, Marcus! It's lovely to see you.' She kissed his cheek. 'And, Cassie, thank you so much for bringing the cake.'

Cassie and Alex smiled. What a brilliant day it was turning into.

I'm sure I can grant Marcus's wish now, Cassie thought.

Marcus carefully placed the cupcake and the mugs for his trick on the table next to the cake box.

'Could you bring these props on to the stage when I do the cupcake trick?' he asked Cassie.

'Of course,' she said.

'Maaaaarcus!' squealed an excited voice.

'Lia!' he said as a girl with long black plaits ran across the lawn and threw herself into his arms. He grinned and spun her round.

'It's my birthday,' she said, her eyes sparkling. 'I'm five!'

'I know,' Marcus said, still grinning. 'Happy birthday.'

'And Mum says you've got a special

70

birthday surprise for me,' she whispered, pointing at the stage. 'What is it? Please tell me. I'm so excited I'm nearly bursting!'

Cassie, Alex and Marcus laughed.

Just then Mrs Chen clapped her hands. 'Could all the children come and sit in front of the stage, please,' she said. 'We have a special birthday treat for Lia – a magic show!'

'Hooray!' Lia cried. 'I can't wait to see Marcus's tricks!' She settled down in front of the stage with her friends.

'Good luck,' Alex told Marcus.

'You'll be great,' Cassie added. 'After all, you're the Great Fandango.'

Marcus smiled nervously and went behind the stage curtains to get ready.

Cassie and Alex joined the children to
watch the show.
Cassie could feel
butterflies dancing
in her tummy.

*If anything goes
wrong*, Cassie
thought, *I'll find
a way to help him.
I must make sure
his wish comes true!*

'Ladies and gentlemen, girls and boys,'
announced Mrs Chen, 'please welcome the
Great Fandango!'

She pulled a cord and the red
curtains swept open to reveal Marcus in
his magician's cape and hat. Everyone

72

cheered, Lia loudest of all.

Marcus bowed. 'For my first trick—' he began.

But a screeching voice interrupted. 'I want to do my acrobatic act!'

Cassie looked round to see Donna Fox marching out of the hotel and towards the stage, her parents following.

'But, sweetums, they have an act already,' Donna's father said.

'You promised,' said Donna, her voice rising.

'Yes, of course,' her mother agreed. 'Mrs Chen, would you mind letting Donna do her act first?'

'Of course she doesn't mind,' Donna said. 'I will be BRILLIANT.'

With that, she leaped on to the stage, doing cartwheels and forward rolls. She didn't pay any attention at all to Marcus, who scooted out of the way in surprise.

Poor Marcus, thought Cassie. *That Donna is such a show-off! I must stop her spoiling Lia's birthday.*

Cassie stood up. But too late! Donna cartwheeled right into one of the poles that held up the stage curtain. It toppled sideways on to the cake table, dragging the curtain with it.

Squelch! The beautiful fairy-castle birthday cake was squashed under the pole – as well as Marcus's cupcake.

Lia burst into tears. Up on the stage, Donna took a bow. Cassie saw her give

Marcus a smug little
smile. His act was ruined.

If only Donna had been splattered with icing,
Cassie thought crossly. *Then she wouldn't look
so pleased with herself!*

To Cassie's amazement, her flower charm
started to tingle, then burst into a bunch of

flowers. As Donna skipped past the table, the squashed birthday cake smashed on to the ground by her feet – sending up a spray of gooey icing. It covered Donna's costume and face in gooey drips! She shrieked in horror.

Oh dear! Cassie thought.

Lia stopped crying and burst out laughing. The other children laughed along with her. Cassie couldn't help thinking that Donna did look

76

very funny covered in
sticky icing. But then
she saw Marcus in his
magician's cape and
hat, looking sad.

This is terrible,
Cassie thought. *How
am I going to help Marcus now?*

7
Magical Birthday Party

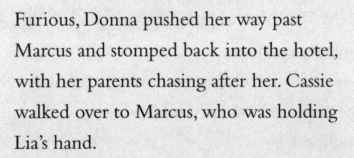

Furious, Donna pushed her way past
Marcus and stomped back into the hotel,
with her parents chasing after her. Cassie
walked over to Marcus, who was holding
Lia's hand.

'I can't do my magic show,' said Marcus,
showing Cassie the squashed cupcake.
'Sorry you can't have your birthday surprise
now, Lia.'

'Thanks anyway, Marcus,' Lia said. 'I'm

just happy you came to my party.'

Cassie thought how brave Lia was trying to be. She looked at where Mrs Chen was clearing up the mess made by the ruined birthday cake, and had an idea.

Perhaps I can make Marcus's wish come true after all, she thought.

'Marcus,' she said quietly, 'you can still do your magic show.'

'But how will I do the ending without the cupcake?' asked Marcus, looking confused.

Cassie glanced around and spotted Alex helping to set up the lucky-dip game, taking the last parcel out of a box covered in silvery paper. Under the trestle table she saw the empty box from the Fairy-cake Bakery

80

and a stripy box for the balloons and banner.

'Just leave the ending to me,' she said brightly. 'I promise it will work out – trust me!'

Marcus still looked a bit worried.

Cassie straightened his black cape. 'Remember, the Great Fandango never gives up,' she said gently.

Cassie picked up the cake box and the stripy box, then joined Alex.

'Can I borrow this?'

she asked, pointing to the silver box.

'Of course,' Alex said. 'What are you going to do?'

'A very special probability trick,' Cassie replied.

She and Marcus climbed on to the stage. With some help from Mrs Chen, they managed to fix the red curtain back on to the pole.

'Ready?' said Cassie.

Marcus nodded.

'Can you all take your seats again, please,' Mrs Chen called to the children. 'The Great Fandango will continue his magic show.'

Lia and her friends cheered. Cassie watched from behind the curtain. Soon, everyone was holding their sides with

The Birthday Wish

laughter. Marcus
lost the scarves
in the scarf trick
again and then
produced a dozen
eggs from out of
his sleeve while
clucking loudly
like a hen.
The
children clapped and roared with laughter.

'Boys and girls,' Marcus said, 'that's nearly
the end of my magic show.'

The children groaned.

'But I have one last trick,' he said. 'Do you
want to see it?'

The children cheered.

Marcus walked over to Cassie. 'What do I do now?' he whispered as she passed him the boxes.

'You're going to make a birthday cake appear in one of the boxes,' Cassie replied.

'I am?' Marcus said, nervously.

'You're the Great Fandango,' Cassie said. 'All you have to do is believe in birthday magic.'

Marcus nodded and turned back to the audience. 'Boys and girls,' he said, 'for my final trick I will make a birthday cake appear in one of these boxes.'

The Birthday Wish

He placed the cake box upside down on the stage, then the stripy box and the silver box.

I hope this works, Cassie thought, crossing her fingers.

'I need a helper from the audience,' Marcus said, pointing to Lia.

Smiling, she walked on to the stage.

Marcus handed her his wand. 'Please wave the wand over the boxes,' he said.

Lia waved the wand.

'Now choose the box you think the cake is in,' he said.

Lia picked up the silver box. Her face fell. 'There's nothing there,' she said.

Marcus opened his eyes wide in a funny surprised face, tossed the box in the air and

made it land on his head like a wonky hat. Lia chuckled.

Next, Lia picked the stripy box. Nothing was under it.

Marcus walked slowly towards the cake box. Behind the curtain, Cassie concentrated hard on the flower charm. *Please make a beautiful birthday cake appear*, she thought. Silver sparkles swirled around her bracelet and she felt the tingling sensation go up her arm.

The Birthday Wish

On her wrist, the flower charm burst into a bouquet!

Marcus picked up the cake box. The audience gasped. A beautiful cake stood on the stage. It had a fairy castle and sugar fairies, just like before, and sparkled with edible glitter.

Lia's eyes shone. 'Oh, Marcus, thank you!' she said. 'You're the best. And this is the best birthday ever!'

'Hooray!' Cassie cheered along with everyone else. Then she felt another tingle on her wrist. With a swirl of shimmering stars, a beautiful cupcake charm appeared. She had done it. She had granted Marcus's wish — with his magic show, he had made Lia's birthday extra-special. And now Cassie

had earned another magical charm!

'You're the greatest magician in the world,' Lia said, hugging Marcus tightly.

'You really are,' Mrs Chen said, joining them. 'I have no idea how you did that trick, Marcus. Where did the cake come from?'

Marcus looked at Cassie.

'A great magician never reveals his secrets,' she said.

'I don't know how it happened either,' added Marcus, 'but it goes to show that if you believe in magic anything is possible.'

Cassie and Alex grinned at each other.

That night, Cassie floated through the open panel in the domed glass roof of her

bedroom. Silvery
stars spiralled
from her
bird charm
and swirled
around her. In
her hand, she
had a gift for a
special friend.

The sky was
filled with stars, but
Cassie flew straight towards the star that
glowed the brightest of all. As she got closer,
it grew into a column of dazzling light, and
changed into Stella Starkeeper.

'Hello, Stella!' said Cassie. 'Look, I've got a
new charm!'

The Birthday Wish

She held up her wrist so Stella could see the cupcake charm on her bracelet. It had pink icing and a cherry on top.

'I'm so pleased,' Stella said. Her eyes sparkled. 'You only have two more charms to earn and you'll be a fully fledged Lucky Star!'

Cassie sighed. 'I can't wait,' she said. 'But I can't quite control my magic yet. I covered poor Donna Fox in icing!'

Stella gave Cassie a hug. 'It isn't easy, becoming a Lucky Star, but I know you can do it.'

'I've brought something for you,' Cassie said, 'as a thank you for always believing in me.'

She held out a cupcake, all the way from the Fairy-cake Bakery. On the top, in bright yellow icing, were the initials 'SS' for Stella Starkeeper.

The Birthday Wish

'Delicious,' Stella said, taking a bite. 'It's magical, just like your new charm!'

Cassie looked at the little cupcake charm on her bracelet.

Whose wish will I grant next? she wondered. *And what magical adventures will I have?*

Cassie's Things to Make and Do!

Join in the Lucky Stars fun!

The Birthday Wish Crossword

Can you find the answers to the questions below and fit them into this crossword? The answers are all from the story you've just read. Good luck!

Down:

1. What does my friend Alex want to be when he grows up?

3. _____ Manor Hotel is the name of the hotel where Lia's birthday was being held and where snooty Donna Fox lives?

4. What is the first name of our new friend, otherwise known as the Great Fandango?

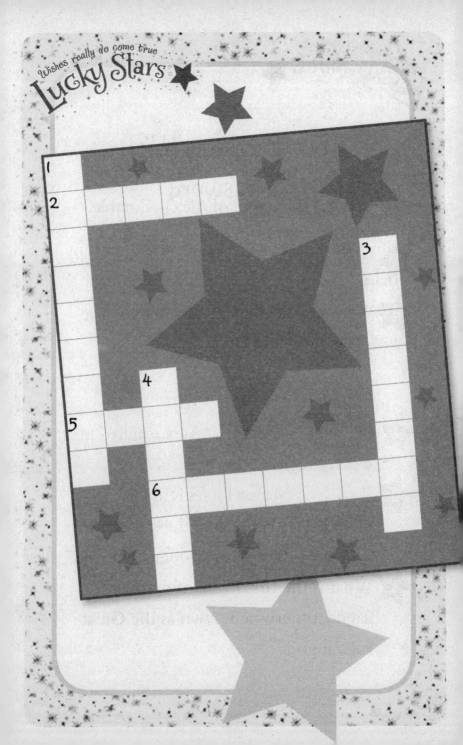

Across:

2. What is the name of Alex's adorable white puppy?

5. What game am I playing with Alex at the start of the story?

6. What charm did I get for helping the Great Fandango?

Strawberry Cupcakes!

Ingredients

10 tablespoons of soft butter

¾ cup white sugar

3 eggs

2 teaspoons red or pink food dye

1¾ cups self-raising flour

¼ cup finely chopped fresh strawberries

1½ cups of icing sugar

3 tablespoons of water

Sprinkles, sweets or strawberries to decorate

Making time:
15 mins
Cooking time:
20 mins
Ready to eat in:
1 hr 35 mins

How to Make

1. Ask an adult to help you with the oven! Preheat the oven to 165 degrees Celsius or Gas Mark 3.

2. Use some butter or sunflower oil to grease a twelve-pocket cupcake tray or place paper cupcake cases in each pocket.

3. In a large bowl, mix the butter and white sugar until light and fluffy. Beat in the eggs one at a time, and then stir in one teaspoon of red or pink food dye. Add the self-raising flour and stir into the mixture until just blended. Fold in the fresh strawberries last. Then carefully spoon the batter into the prepared cups, dividing evenly.

4. Ask an adult to help you place them in the preheated oven. When the tops spring back when lightly pressed, they are done. This should take roughly twenty to twenty-five minutes.

5. Let them cool in the cupcake tray on a wire rack. When cool, arrange the cupcakes on a plate.

6. Now mix the icing sugar and the rest of the food dye with three tablespoons of water. Spread the icing on the top of each cake and add your sprinkles or sweets.

The Birthday Wish Crossword

Answers

Don't look unless you're really stuck!

Lucky Stars

Wishes really do come true

Wishes really do come true
Lucky Stars

The Film Star Wish

To read an exciting chapter,

please turn the page . . .

1
Strawberries and Sparkles

Cassie Cafferty was the only early-morning customer at Farmer Greg's 'pick your own' fruit farm. Hundreds of ripe red strawberries still dotted the lush green plants, but her basket was full.

Cassie picked one last giant berry and popped it in her mouth. So juicy!

At the checkout, Farmer Greg said cheerily, 'Hello, young Cassie. Goodness, you've got enough strawberries here for

everyone in Astral-on-
Sea!'

'Mum's making
strawberry meringues as
a treat for the guests
at Starwatcher
Towers,' said
Cassie.

'It's a busy life, running a bed and
breakfast, I'm sure,' said Farmer Greg.

'You're right,' said Cassie. She paid and
took her basket. The scent from the sun-
warmed fruit was sweet. 'Mmmm!' she said.
'The guests will love these. Bye!'

Cassie headed along the edge of Whimsy
Wood. There were a few dog-walkers
about, but otherwise she had the path to

herself. She swung her basket as she went,
being careful not to lose any strawberries.

Something in the wood caught Cassie's
eye. She peered among the trees. Sunlight
dappled the leaves but, further in among the
shadows, there was . . . yes! It was an orb of
silver light, like a fallen star.

Cassie smiled. *Could that light be Stella
Starkeeper?* she wondered. She hoped it was!

As Cassie pulled a branch aside, the
charms on her silver bracelet tinkled. Stella
Starkeeper had given her the bracelet on
her seventh birthday, a few weeks ago. It
held a magical secret!

Each charm gave Cassie a special power.
Whenever she helped make someone's
wish come true, she received a new charm.

Lucky Stars

Once she received seven charms, she would become a Lucky Star. So far she had five. The little bird gave her the power to fly, and the crescent moon helped her to talk to animals. With the silver butterfly she could stop time, and with the flower charm she could make things appear.

Cassie's newest charm was a cute cupcake, but she and her friend, Alex, still hadn't discovered its power. Alex was the only other person who knew about the magical charms – apart from Stella, of course. Alex was staying at Starwatcher Towers for a couple of weeks with his parents and his puppy, Comet. He and Cassie had become firm friends.

Cassie watched the silver light dance further into the trees.

'It's going!' she gasped. 'I must see if it really is Stella!' She chased the light, but it moved too swiftly.

Cassie realized she needed the bracelet's magical power if she was to catch it up. She concentrated hard on her bird charm. Her wrist tingled. Sparkles swirled from the bracelet, then spiralled around her.

Cassie rose off the ground and flew after the light. She moved quickly through the trees, clutching her basket carefully so it wouldn't get caught on a branch.

The light continued along the deserted

main path through Whimsy Wood, straight towards Astral-on-Sea's open-air cinema.

In a few moments, Cassie reached the clearing. A giant screen was set up. There were rows of benches on which to sit, and a large grassy area where families could have a picnic. During film screenings, refreshments were sold at the kiosk that stood to one side.

Cassie spotted the silver light twinkling

in front of a poster:

That sounds interesting,
thought Cassie as she drifted
gently to the ground.

Suddenly the light burst
into thousands of tiny sparkles that swirled
towards her. Then, with a *shoosh* and a
whoosh and a *whizz-fizz-fizz*, the sparkles
gathered into a dazzling column of light.

Cassie's heart skipped a beat as the light
changed into a lovely young woman with
long fair hair. She held a wand, tipped with
a twinkling star, and all her clothes were
silver. She wore glittery leggings and glossy
boots beneath a silky dress that rippled in
the breeze. Star-shaped buttons glittered on
the cuffs of her shiny cropped jacket, and

she wore a glistening crown, woven from the finest silver strands.

The woman smiled and her velvety-blue eyes twinkled.

'Hello, Stella!' cried Cassie, running to hug her.

'What a lovely welcome,' Stella said in her soft, warm voice. 'And what wonderful strawberries.'

'Try them!' said Cassie.

Stella took one. 'It's heart-shaped!' she said. Then she tasted it. 'Mmm, so sweet!' She touched Cassie's bracelet with her wand. 'You have earned five charms already.'

Cassie nodded. 'If I earn two more,' she said, 'I'll become a true Lucky Star, like you.'

'Yes, and then you can grant any wish

you like, as long as you feel it's right. But until then you must listen carefully to my clues and to hear the right wish.' She smiled. 'Do you like your new cupcake charm?'

'It's lovely,' said Cassie, 'but I don't know what power it has. Can you tell me?' she asked. 'Or maybe give me a clue?'

Stella raised her wand above Cassie. Brilliant light shone down from it to form a shining pool.

Cassie felt as if she was standing in a spotlight. She twirled like a ballerina. 'Do I look like a star onstage?' she asked, laughing.

Stella smiled. 'Not everybody enjoys being in the spotlight, Cassie.' She popped another heart-shaped strawberry into her mouth. Then, with a wave of her wand, she

vanished behind a veil
of silvery sparkles.

As the sparkles
drifted away, Cassie
turned towards
home, thinking
over what Stella
had said.

'*Not everybody enjoys
being in the spotlight . . .*'

Was it a clue? If so,
whatever could it mean?

Wishes really do come true
Lucky Stars

Explore the magical world of Lucky Stars!

For fun things to make and do – as well as games and quizzes – go to:

www.luckystarsbooks.co.uk

Wishes really do come true
Lucky Stars

Cassie is training to become a Lucky Star –
someone who can make wishes come true!
Follow her on more exciting adventures as
she meets new friends in need of help.

www.luckystarsbooks.co.uk